Fruits
of the
Spirit

A 40 DAY READING GUIDE AND PRAYER JOURNAL

ASHLEY BUFE

Fruits of the Spirit: A daily reading schedule and journal.

Copyright © by Ashley Bufe

Scriptures taken from *The Holy Bible, King James Version*. Cambridge
Edition: 1769; *King James Bible Online*, 2019.
www.kingjamesbibleonline.org.

Find Ashley here:
Blog: www.myhousefullofboys.com
Facebook: www.facebook.com/myhousefullboys
Instagram: www.instagram.com/myhousefullofboysblog
Email: myhousefullofboys@gmail.com

This daily Bible reading guide and journal is a great way to spend some time in the Word reflecting on the Fruits of the Spirit.

Included are:
- A brief overview and beautiful memory verse coloring page for each fruit.
- A daily reading guide that covers a fruit of the Spirit.
- A prayer journal designed to help the reader become intentional about how they can serve and pray for themselves and others.
- A follow-up to reflect on your own personal walk.

How to use this book:
This is a 40 day study. There are 10 sections- fruits, love, joy, peace, longsuffering, gentleness, goodness, faith, meekness, and temperance. Each section has one day of an overview and memory verse, and 3 days of guided reading and prayer journaling.

It is my prayer that this guide can be a blessing to all who use it. And that through this guide, we may see how important it is to bear good fruit, and how the Spirit can help us do just that.

I would love for you to share this with your friends, families, and churches, and leave me a review on Amazon.

If you are interested in bulk prices, or purchasing additional journals, please search for me on Amazon, or email me.

-Ashley

DAY 1

Genesis 3 is one of the earliest mentions of fruit in the Bible, but fruit is something we see mentioned time and time again.

"But the fruit of the Spirit is love, joy, peace, longsuffering, gentleness, goodness, faith, meekness, temperance: against such there is no law." Gal 5:22-23

Think about what Spiritual fruits you bear. Both good and bad. Now, write them down and then spend some time focusing on ways you can water the good fruits and prune the bad.

Read:
Matthew 7:15-20
Luke 8:4-18

BUT THE

Fruit of the Spirit

IS

love

JOY

peace

LONGSUFFERING

gentleness

goodness

meekness

faith

TEMPERANCE

AGAINST SUCH THERE IS NO LAW.

Galatians 5:22-23

DAY 2

Of the Spirit

- John 14:15-24

- Romans 8:1-27

- 1 Corinthians 6:19-20

- 2 Corinthians 3:17-18

- Ephesians 3:16-21

Write it out (write your favorite verse from above.)

_____

_____

_____

_____

I am praying for....

_____

_____

I will share
Jesus with

_____
_____

How? _____
_____

Thank you
God for

_____
_____
_____
_____
_____
_____

Be Intentional Journal

I am working on

_____
_____
_____

Answered prayers

_____

_____

DAY 3

Bear good fruit

- **Numbers 17**

- **Jeremiah 17:5-8**

- **Matthew 13:1-23**

- **Luke 6:43-45**

Write it out (write your favorite verse from above.)

_____

_____

_____

_____

I am praying for....

_____

_____

```
I will share        Thank you
Jesus with          God for

_____           _____
_____           _____
How? _____        _____
_____           _____
                    _____
                    _____
```

Be Intentional Journal

I am working on

_____

_____

_____

Answered prayers

_____

_____

DAY 4

Prune the bad

- Luke 13:1-9

- John 15:1-18

- Galatians 5:13-26

- Galatians 6:7-8

- Ephesians 5:1-20

Write it out (write your favorite verse from above.)

_____

_____

_____

_____

I am praying for...

_____

_____

I will share Jesus with

_____
_____
_____

How? _____
_____

Thank you God for

_____
_____
_____
_____
_____
_____

I am working on

_____
_____
_____

Answered prayers

_____

_____

Be Intentional Journal

It is no surprise that love is the fruit listed first. Love is both the first and second greatest commandments.

Today, read 1 Corinthians 13 and as you read, replace the word "love" with the word "God."

Now, read it again, this time replacing the word "love" with the phrase "I will be." Keep in mind, that this Biblical love is a choice, not a feeling.

Finish today by reading:
Psalm 136
1 John 4:7-21

BELOVED
LET US

love one another;
FOR LOVE IS OF GOD;
AND EVERY ONE THAT

loveth

IS BORN OF GOD,

AND KNOWETH

God.

1 John 4:7

DAY 6

Love the Lord your God

- **Matthew 22:36-40**

- **Exodus 20:1-17**

- **Deuteronomy 6:4-9**

- **Matthew 7:21-27**

- **Romans 8:28**

Write it out (write your favorite verse from above.)

_____

_____

_____

_____

love

I am praying for. . .

_____

_____

I will share Jesus with

_____

_____

_____

How? _____

_____

Thank you God for

_____

_____

_____

_____

_____

I am working on

_____

_____

_____

Answered prayers

_____

_____

Be Intentional Journal

love

DAY 7

Love your neighbor as yourself

- **Matthew 5:43-48**

- **Matthew 25:31-46**

- **Luke 10:25-37**

- **John 13:34-35**

- **Philippians 2:1-11**

Write it out (write your favorite verse from above.)

_____

_____

_____

_____

I am praying for...

_____

_____

I will share Jesus with	Thank you God for
_____	_____
_____	_____
_____	_____
How? _____	_____
_____	_____

I am working on

_____

_____

_____

Answered prayers

_____

_____

Be Intentional Journal

DAY 8

The love of God

- Matthew 18:10-14

- Luke 6:32-36

- Luke 15:11-32

- John 3:16

- John 15:9-17

- Romans 5:8

Write it out (write your favorite verse from above.)

_____

_____

_____

_____

love

I am praying for...

_____

_____

I will share Jesus with

_____
_____
_____

How? _____

_____

Thank you God for

_____
_____
_____
_____
_____

I am working on

_____
_____
_____

Answered prayers

_____

_____

Be Intentional Journal

Joy. Isn't this a fruit that we all crave? I know I do. Joy isn't something we can just turn on and off. It is much deeper than that. This kind of Biblical joy comes through the Holy Spirit as we see the beauty of the cross.

Think of a time in your life that you felt this true joy.

Why do you think you experienced this?

Another aspect of joy is rejoicing. What beauty can you see in the world that makes your heart rejoice?

What beauty can you see in His word that makes your heart rejoice?

Read: Psalm 118:24

This is the day which the **LORD** hath made; we will **REJOICE** and be glad in it.

Psalm 118:24

DAY 10

Rejoice

- **Psalm 16:7-11**

- **Psalm 47**

- **Acts 5:41-42**

- **Philippians 4:4, 10-13**

- **1 Peter 1:3-9**

Write it out

_____

_____

_____

_____

_____

_____

I am praying for...

_____

_____

I will share Jesus with

_____
_____
_____

How? _____

_____

Thank you God for

_____
_____
_____
_____
_____
_____

I am working on

_____
_____
_____

Answered prayers

_____

_____

Be Intentional Journal

DAY 11

The joy of the Lord

- **Nehemiah 8:10**

- **Psalm 30:4-5**

- **Luke 15:8-10**

- **Romans 15:13**

Write it out

_____

_____

_____

_____

_____

_____

I am praying for. . .

_____

_____

I will share Jesus with	Thank you God for
_____	_____
_____	_____
How? _____	_____
_____	_____
	_____

I am working on

_____

_____

_____

Answered prayers

_____

_____

Be Intentional Journal

DAY 12

Joy through Christ

- Luke 1:39-45

- John 16:16-24

- Hebrews 12:1-3

- James 1:2-4

Write it out

_____
_____
_____
_____
_____
_____

I am praying for....

_____

_____

```
┌──────────────────┐  ┌──────────────────┐
│  I will share    │  │  Thank you       │
│  Jesus with      │  │  God for         │
│  _____    │  │  _____    │
│  _____    │  │  _____    │
│  How? _____    │  │  _____    │
│  _____    │  │  _____    │
└──────────────────┘  └──────────────────┘
```

I am working on

_____

_____

_____

Answered prayers

_____

_____

Be Intentional Journal

DAY 13

I have never felt a sense of peace like I did in the ICU waiting room while waiting for my 4 week old son to come out of surgery. In these moments, I knew that literally everything was out of my hands. God was completely in control and I knew that I wasn't. My wisdom, knowledge, and power had reached its limit and I had to fully trust the wisdom, knowledge, and power of God.

I truly believe that peace is found in those hard moments when we let go and let God.

Have you ever experienced this peace that passes understanding?

Why do you think you experienced peace in this situation?

Read:
Philippians 4:11-13
Colossians 3:15

AND LET THE

PEACE

of God

rule in your

hearts,

**to the which also ye
are called in one body;**

and

be ye Thankful.

Colossians 3:15

DAY 14

Peace through Christ

- Isaiah 9:6

- John 16:33

- Romans 5:1-11

- Ephesians 2:11-22

- Colossians 1:15-23

- Colossians 3:12-17

Write it out

_____

_____

_____

_____

_____

_____

I am praying for...

_____

_____

I will share Jesus with	Thank you God for
_____	_____
_____	_____
How? _____	_____
_____	_____
	_____

I am working on

_____

_____

_____

Answered prayers

_____

_____

Be Intentional Journal

DAY 15

Peace of God

- **Numbers 6:24-26**

- **Matthew 11:28-30**

- **John 14:25-27**

- **Philippians 4:4-9**

- **1 Thessalonians 5:23-24**

Write it out

_____

_____

_____

_____

_____

_____

I am praying for...

_____

_____

I will share Jesus with

_____
_____
_____

How? _____

_____

Thank you God for

_____
_____
_____
_____
_____
_____

I am working on

_____
_____
_____

Answered prayers

_____

_____

Be Intentional Journal

DAY 16

Peace among men

- **Psalm 34:13-14**

- **Matthew 5:9**

- **1 Thessalonians 5:12-15**

- **Hebrews 12:14**

- **James 3:13-18**

- **1 Peter 3:8-12**

Write it out

_____

_____

_____

_____

_____

_____

I am praying for....

_____

_____

I will share Jesus with	Thank you God for
_____	_____
_____	_____
How? _____	_____
_____	_____

I am working on

_____

_____

_____

Answered prayers

_____

_____

Be Intentional Journal

DAY 17 longsuffering

We live in a world of "now." Instant gratification. Fast paced. Always rushing. Always busy.

There are two different aspects of this fruit-longsuffering and patience. Perseverance, and waiting.

Waiting, for anything really, is hard to do. But waiting is just what we are called to do. Wait on the Lord. Sometimes we may be waiting because God has different plans or different timing. Sometimes we may just be waiting because God knows that through the wait, we will develop a deeper faith, a stronger character, and an unfailing hope.

Longsuffering is often a challenge because it deals with other people. And people aren't perfect.

Both patience and longsuffering are gifts, and both are the result of us yielding to God.

Read: Romans 12:12

Rejoicing in hope; Patient in tribulation; continuing instant in prayer.

Romans 12:12

DAY 18

Wait on the Lord

- **Ecclesiastes 3:1-11**

- **Isaiah 40:25-31**

- **Lamentations 3:25-27**

- **Romans 8:18-27**

- **James 5:7-11**

Write it out

_____

_____

_____

_____

_____

_____

I am praying for....

_____

_____

I will share Jesus with
_____
_____
_____
How? _____
_____

Thank you God for
_____
_____
_____
_____
_____
_____

I am working on

_____
_____
_____

Answered prayers

_____
_____

Be Intentional Journal

Longsuffering

- **Isaiah 43:2-3**

- **Matthew 5:10-12**

- **2 Corinthians 4:7-12**

- **2 Timothy 1:6-13**

- **James 1:2-5**

- **Revelation 21:4**

Write it out

_____

_____

_____

_____

_____

_____

I am praying for...

_____

_____

I will share
Jesus with

_____

_____
_____
How? _____
_____

Thank you
God for

_____
_____
_____
_____
_____
_____

Be Intentional Journal

I am working on

_____

_____

_____

Answered prayers

_____

_____

DAY 20

Patience

- **Psalm 27:14**

- **Psalm 37:7-9**

- **Proverbs 15:18**

- **Romans 12:12**

- **Philippians 4:6**

Write it out

_____

_____

_____

_____

_____

_____

I am praying for...

_____

_____

I will share Jesus with	Thank you God for
_____	_____
_____	_____
How? _____	_____
_____	_____

I am working on

_____

_____

_____

Answered prayers

_____

_____

Be Intentional Journal

DAY 21 *gentleness*

When it comes to gentleness, we have the perfect example. Jesus.

Time and time again, we see Jesus demonstrate great gentleness, kindness, and compassion.

Sometimes it's easy to want to be shown kindness, but much harder to show kindness ourselves. But this fruit is one that God calls us to. And often, we must truly be intentional about it before we will bear it. It takes learning and practice, and it starts with caring and being tenderhearted towards others.

Who is someone you know personally that radiates gentleness? Why do you think this is?

Who is someone that you have a hard time being kind to? How can you focus on being more intentional with showing this person kindness?

Read:
Ephesians 4:31-32

And be ye
K I N D

to one another,
tenderhearted.

forgiving

one

another,

even as God for Christ's sake

hath

forgiven you.

Ephesians 4:32

DAY 22

Gods kindness through Christ

- **Mark 10:13-16**

- **Romans 2:1-4**

- **Romans 11:22-24**

- **Ephesians 2:1-10**

- **Titus 3:3-7**

Write it out (write your favorite verse from above.)

_____

_____

_____

_____

I am praying for....

_____

_____

<table>
<tr>
<td>
I will share
Jesus with

_____
_____
How? _____

_____
</td>
<td>
Thank you
God for

_____
_____
_____
_____
_____
</td>
</tr>
</table>

I am working on

_____

_____

_____

Answered prayers

_____

_____

Be Intentional Journal

The kindness of Christ

- **Matthew 8:1-13**

- **Luke 8:40-56**

- **Luke 17:11-19**

- **Luke 19:1-9**

- **John 9:1-12**

Write it out

_____

_____

_____

_____

_____

_____

I am praying for...

_____

_____

I will share Jesus with

_____
_____
_____

How? _____
_____

Thank you God for

_____
_____
_____
_____
_____
_____

I am working on

_____

_____

_____

Answered prayers

_____

_____

Be Intentional Journal

DAY 24 *gentleness*

Living in gentleness

- **Proverbs 21:21**
- **Matthew 6:1-4**
- **Luke 6:27-36**
- **Ephesians 4:25-32**
- **1 John 3:16-18**

Write it out

_____

_____

_____

_____

_____

_____

I am praying for...

_____

_____

I will share Jesus with

_____
_____
_____

How? _____

_____

Thank you God for

_____
_____
_____
_____
_____

Be Intentional Journal

I am working on

_____

_____

_____

Answered prayers

_____

_____

DAY 25

The fruit of goodness isn't only just a behavior. Its not just something we can make ourselves do. It is a characteristic of God and it comes from Him.

Our goodness begins by loving God. And we only obtain it through God's power as He works in our hearts.

We are called to bear fruit. To allow the Spirit to lead us to doing. Goodness is virtue, righteousness, truth, and love in action.

Read:
James 1:17
Matthew 5:6
3 John 1:11

Let your light so **shine** BEFORE MEN, THAT THEY MAY SEE YOUR *good works,* AND GLORIFY YOUR FATHER WHICH IS IN HEAVEN.

Matthew 5:16

DAY 26

Do good

- Galatians 6:1-10

- Ephesians 2:8-10

- Hebrews 10:23-25

- 3 John 1:11-12

Write it out

_____

_____

_____

_____

_____

_____

I am praying for...

_____

_____

I will share Jesus with
_____
_____
How? _____
_____

Thank you God for
_____
_____
_____
_____

I am working on
_____
_____
_____

Answered prayers

_____

_____

Be Intentional Journal

DAY 27

gods goodness

- **Psalm 23**

- **Psalm 31:19-20**

- **Psalm 34:8**

- **Psalm 145:9-21**

- **James 1:16-18**

Write it out

_____

_____

_____

_____

_____

_____

I am praying for....

_____

_____

I will share Jesus with

_____
_____
_____

How? _____
_____

Thank you God for

_____
_____
_____
_____
_____
_____

I am working on

_____
_____
_____

Answered prayers

_____
_____

Be Intentional Journal

DAY 28

And it was good

- **Genesis 1**

Write it out

_____

_____

_____

_____

_____

_____

I am praying for....

_____

_____

I will share Jesus with	Thank you God for
_____	_____
_____	_____
How? _____	_____
_____	_____
	_____

I am working on

_____

_____

_____

Answered prayers

_____

_____

Be Intentional Journal

The Bible is full of men and women of faith. The stories of Noah, Abraham and Isaac, David and Goliath, Gideon, Joshua, and Esther show us what strong faith looks like, just to name a few.

Like many of these mentioned, our faith is often put to the test when we are in the middle of a storm.

We are called to live by faith. And the fruit of faith leads to action.

Can you think of a time in your life when you were enduring a trial and your faith helped you get through?

What about a time when your faith led to action?

Read: Gideon's story in Judges 7

Trust

IN THE

Lord

with all thine

heart

AND LEAN NOT UNTO THINE OWN UNDERSTANDING.

In all thy ways acknowledge him,

and he shall direct Thy paths.

Proverbs 3:5-6

DAY 30

He is faithful

- **1 Corinthians 1:4-9**

- **1 Corinthians 10:11-13**

- **2 Thessalonians 3:1-5**

- **2 Timothy 2:8-13**

- **1 John 1:5-10**

Write it out

_____

_____

_____

_____

_____

_____

I am praying for...

_____

_____

I will share Jesus with	Thank you God for
_____	_____
_____	_____
How? _____	_____
_____	_____

Be Intentional Journal

I am working on

_____

_____

_____

Answered prayers

_____

_____

DAY 31 faithfulness

Righteousness through faith

- **Proverbs 3:1-6**

- **Luke 17:1-19**

- **Romans 3:21-31**

- **Romans 4:13-25**

- **James 5:13-20**

Write it out (write your favorite verse from above.)

_____

_____

_____

_____

I am praying for....

_____

_____

I will share Jesus with
_____
_____
How? _____
_____

Thank you God for
_____
_____
_____
_____

I am working on
_____
_____
_____

Answered prayers

_____

_____

Be Intentional Journal

DAY 32

faithfulness

Hall of Faith

- Hebrews 10:19-39

- Hebrews 11

- Hebrews 12:1-3

Write it out (write your favorite verse from above.)

_____

_____

_____

_____

I am praying for....

_____

_____

I will share Jesus with	Thank you God for
_____	_____
_____	_____
How? _____	_____
_____	_____

Be Intentional Journal

I am working on

_____

_____

_____

Answered prayers

_____

_____

DAY 33

So often in our world today, meekness and humility are mistaken for weakness. But the opposite is true. Those who humble themselves show great strength.

Jesus was approachable, lowly, and humble. He was a servant. Yet he was powerful.

This fruit is similar to gentleness. Gentleness however mainly involves our actions, whereas meekness involves our attitude as well as our actions.

Think of some times when Jesus demonstrated meekness. How can you do the same?

Read:
James 1:19-21
Psalm 37

With all lowliness

and meekness

With
longsuffering

FORBEARING ONE
ANOTHER IN LOVE

Ephesians 4:2

DAY 34 *meekness*

Humble yourself

- **Galatians 6:1-5**

- **Ephesians 4:1-6**

- **2 Timothy 2:22-26**

- **James 4:6-10**

- **1 Peter 5:5-11**

Write it out

_____

_____

_____

_____

_____

_____

I am praying for...

_____

_____

I will share Jesus with	Thank you God for
_____	_____
_____	_____
How? _____	_____
_____	_____

I am working on

_____

_____

_____

Answered prayers

_____

_____

Be Intentional Journal

DAY 35

The meekness of Christ

- **Matthew 20:25-28**

- **Matthew 21:1-11**

- **John 13:1-17**

- **2 Corinthians 8:8-9**

- **Philippians 2:1-11**

Write it out

_____

_____

_____

_____

_____

_____

I am praying for. . .

_____

_____

I will share Jesus with

_____
_____
_____

How? _____

_____

Thank you God for

_____
_____
_____
_____
_____

I am working on

_____
_____
_____

Answered prayers

_____

_____

Be Intentional Journal

DAY 36

Humility

- Luke 7:36-50

- Luke 14:7-14

- Romans 12:16

- 2 Corinthians 12:9-10

- 1 Peter 3:1-7

Write it out

_____

_____

_____

_____

_____

_____

I am praying for...

_____

_____

I will share Jesus with	Thank you God for
_____	_____
_____	_____
_____	_____
How? _____	_____
_____	_____

Be Intentional Journal

I am working on

_____

_____

_____

Answered prayers

_____

_____

DAY 37

Temperance, by definition, is restraint or moderation of actions, words, and thoughts. Another word for it is self-control.

When we are filled with the Spirit, we put away our fleshly desires. We have self-control.

This fruit is a very challenging one, because it is in direct opposition with our worldly passions.

When we live self-controlled lives, we are better equipped to represent Christ. In what aspects of your life do you find it challenging to practice self-control?

Make a game plan today to help you overcome those temptations.

Read:
James 4:7
1 Corinthians 9:27
1 Corinthians 10:31
Romans 13:14

And be not conformed to this world:

BUT BE YE

transformed

BY THE renewing

OF YOUR MIND, that ye may prove good, and what is that acceptable, and perfect, WILL OF GOD

Romans 12:2

DAY 38 temperance

Stand firm

- Luke 9:23-26

- Ephesians 6:10-20

- Titus 2

- James 4:1-12

- 1 John 2:15-17

Write it out

_____
_____
_____
_____
_____
_____

I am praying for....

_____

_____

I will share Jesus with

_____

_____

How? _____

_____

Thank you God for

_____

_____

_____

_____

I am working on

_____

_____

_____

Answered prayers

_____

_____

Be Intentional Journal

temperance

Fleshly desires

- **Romans 8:12-17**

- **1 Corinthians 6:12-20**

- **1 Corinthians 9:24-27**

- **Galatians 5:13-26**

- **Ephesians 5:3-20**

Write it out

_____

_____

_____

_____

_____

_____

I am praying for....

_____

_____

I will share Jesus with	Thank you God for
_____	_____
_____	_____
How? _____	_____
_____	_____

Be Intentional Journal

I am working on

_____

_____

_____

Answered prayers

_____

_____

DAY 40 Temperance

Of the mind

- **Matthew 4:1-11**

- **Romans 12:1-2**

- **Philippians 4:8-9**

- **James 1:19-27**

Write it out

_____

_____

_____

_____

_____

_____

I am praying for....

_____

_____

I will share Jesus with

_____

_____

How? _____

_____

Thank you God for

_____

_____

_____

_____

I am working on

_____

_____

_____

Answered prayers

_____

_____

Be Intentional Journal

Follow-up

Go through the fruits and list the three that come easiest for you.

1._____
2._____
3._____

Why do you think these fruits come easiest for you?

_____
_____
_____
_____

When in your life have you put these fruits to use?

_____
_____
_____
_____

How do you use these fruits in your daily life?

_____
_____
_____
_____

I am praying for...

_____

_____

I will share Jesus with	Thank you God for
_____	_____
_____	_____
How? _____	_____
_____	_____
	_____

Be Intentional Journal

I am working on

_____

_____

_____

Answered prayers

_____

_____

Follow-up

Go through the fruits and list the three that are hardest for you.

1._____
2._____
3._____

Why do you think these fruits are the hardest?

_____
_____
_____
_____

Can you think of any specific times in your life when you didn't bear these fruits?

_____
_____
_____
_____

How can you be more intentional about bearing these fruits?

_____
_____
_____
_____

I am praying for...

_____

_____

I will share Jesus with	Thank you, God, for
_____	_____
_____	_____
How? _____	_____
_____	_____
	_____

I am working on

_____

_____

_____

Answered prayers

_____

_____

Be Intentional Journal

Notes

Notes

Notes

Notes

I am praying for...

_____

_____

I will share
Jesus with

_____

_____

How? _____

_____

Thank you,
God, for

_____

_____

_____

_____

_____

Be Intentional Journal

I am working on

_____

_____

_____

Answered prayers

_____

_____

I am praying for....

_____

_____

I will share Jesus with	Thank you, God, for
_____	_____
_____	_____
How? _____	_____
_____	_____
	_____

I am working on

_____

_____

_____

Answered prayers

_____

_____

Be Intentional Journal

I am praying for...

_____

_____

I will share Jesus with

_____

_____

How? _____

_____

Thank you, God, for

_____

_____

_____

_____

_____

_____

I am working on

_____

_____

_____

Answered prayers

_____

_____

Be Intentional Journal

I am praying for. . .

_____

_____

I will share Jesus with	Thank you, God, for
_____	_____
_____	_____
How? _____	_____
_____	_____

I am working on

_____

_____

_____

Answered prayers

_____

_____

Be Intentional Journal

Made in the USA
Las Vegas, NV
01 November 2021